# How Does it Feel to be One of the Beautiful People?

Napoleon Esteban

Books Academy LLC
112 SW H K Dodgen Loop, Temple, Texas 76504
Hotline: (254) 800-1189

Ordering Information:
Quantity sales. Special discounts are available on quantity purchases by corporations, associations, and others. For details, contact the publisher at the address above.

Printed in the United States of America.

| ISBN-13: | Softcover | 978-1-966567-74-5 |
| | Hardbound | 978-1-966567-76-9 |
| | eBook | 978-1-966567-75-2 |

Library of Congress Control Number: 2025909582

# INTRODUCTION

*TRUTH IS BEAUTY, BEAUTY IS TRUTH. THAT IS ALL WE KNOW, AND ALL WE NEED TO KNOW.* **– JOHN KEATS**

Imagine living in a world where everything is beautiful. You wake up each day to blue skies, the sun shining, and the birds are all singing sweet melodies. The weather is always perfect and you're thankful to be alive.

On the day of creation, the Gods said, "Let US create man in OUR image." There was no darkness. We had been created in a way that we were led by The Spirit. There was no such thing as ego, greed, jealousy, envy, or hatred. As Human Beings we understood our purpose was to lift each other up.

We treated each other with love and respect without ever expecting anything in return. There was no concern about doing the right thing so we could go to heaven. Instead, we did the right thing to enjoy this heaven on earth.

The outward appearance of man did not matter, for we were more concerned about the substance of one's character. There was never a need to try to look attractive. In our hearts we know we are all beautiful creations.

Pity the poor soul who has become insecure for feeling inadequate to today's new standard of beauty. Pity the poor soul who continuously cries out, "Look at ME!"

# EYES THAT SEE THE TRUTH

They say the eyes are the windows to the world. With these eyes, I have been able to see the true hearts of men. Sometimes, it hurts to see what they reveal. Many who have portrayed themselves as one of the "Beautiful People" somehow show me who they really are. It scares me to know that people can fool others into not seeing their true selves.

We are who we truly are when we think no one else is watching.

We profess to believe in God, but we don't believe He's watching. I will never claim to be more than a human being—capable of making mistakes and acknowledging them. It's a crying shame when pride overrides humility.

I am not one of the Beautiful People.

ESTEBAN

# A TESTED HEART

"There will come a day when the hearts of men shall be tested." These are the words I once spoke. I didn't think they would ever apply to me. Many consider me a Man of God. If that were true, then when that day came, I should have been led by the Spirit to do what is right.

I had a friend who loved and respected me for how I loved God. He expressed that love through a painting he did of me—a gift from the heart, capturing what he saw as God's calling on my life. But sometimes, we must ask ourselves if we are truly following God's will, or just our own.

After he gave me this heartfelt gift, for some reason, I couldn't thank him or give him any feedback. Even if I didn't like the painting, I could have at least shown some gratitude. He and I both understood the importance of feedback, yet no matter how many times he asked, I refused to respond. I don't know why I was so determined to ignore his genuine expression.

Worse than that—I made him feel like he didn't belong. At a monthly pastoral luncheon I was in charge of, he attended as a representative of his church. He wasn't a pastor. When the event ended, I asked all the pastors to stand. Then I asked the co-pastors to stand. I continued calling on ministry titles until the only person still sitting... was my friend. I wanted him to feel excluded. I wanted to send a message that he didn't belong.

I'm sure that made him feel great.

Yes, I am one of the Beautiful People—the kind who have no problem stepping on someone who shows they care.

ESTEBAN

# PRAISE ME

Let all the saints say, "Amen." Just look at me—you can see how godly I am. I even believe we should be taxed for breathing. I ask, "Would a man rob God?" And all the while, what I really want is praise.

Praise me, for I am a representative of the Most High.

Look into my eyes and see beauty. Believe my words, for I am His Anointed. Follow me... and I'll lead you straight to Hell.

One day, my car broke down on a busy highway. Instead of accepting help, I got out and started praying over it. I kept praying, waiting for a miracle. After a couple of hours, I gave in and called a tow truck.

# THE SPIRITUAL QUEEN

I've always wanted to be one of the Beautiful People. I love when others look at me and wish they had what I possess. I call myself a spiritual Queen and believe I deserve the best this world can offer.

But in truth, I pretend to be holy and wise, when I'm really a parasite—always looking for someone to feed off. I might not even like you, but if there's a free meal involved, I'll tolerate you until dessert.

When I was born, God broke the mold. I am beautifully unique... and beautifully fake.

ESTEBAN

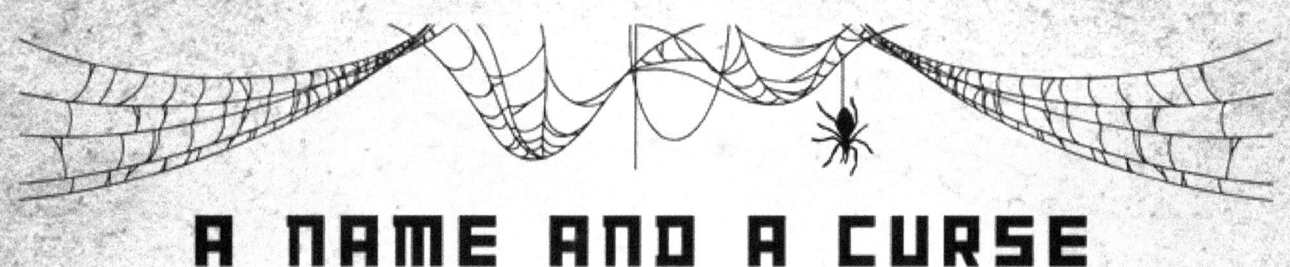

# A NAME AND A CURSE

This is me and my beautiful wife. We have two beautiful children. I have very little knowledge of the spiritual world. Actually, I used to think it was a lot of bologna—until recently.

I got involved in a situation between my adopted father and his older brother. Not knowing the full story, I stood up for my father and cursed out his brother. I didn't realize how wrong I was. I cursed this man—and then gave my children his name.

What I didn't know at the time was that he and my father weren't even blood relatives.

Now I ask myself... is it possible I placed a curse on my own children by dishonoring their true bloodline?

I guess we'll have to wait and see.

We call ourselves Beautiful People. I think.

# CALL ME BEAUTIFUL

Am I not one of the most beautiful women you've ever laid eyes on? I'm also very sexy. I have big brown bedroom eyes, full rosy lips, and two deep dimples. My body is to die for. I have so many admirers, I've lost count.

Whenever I walk into a room, all eyes are on me—they better be! If they're not, I'll put a spell on them. Look into my eyes and fall deep in love with me. I'll make you forget every woman you've ever known... even your own mother.

I'm so sweet, sugar wouldn't melt in my mouth. Please, just say my name... and call me Beautiful.

ESTEBAN

# SISTERS OF DESIRE

We are loving sisters... looking for someone we can devour. Don't be afraid of our beauty—we've been blessed from above. Why don't you come back with us? We'll show you a time you'll never forget.

Turn out the lights and journey with us... to the other side.

ESTEBAN

# THE BEAUTY MAKER

All my life, I've loved making people beautiful. That's why I became a makeup artist. People love looking in the mirror—and I love making them love what they see.

I've been in several commercials—people are drawn to my dark kind of beauty.

Don't you wish you looked this good?

I recently met a new man who loves me to death. But I don't understand why he won't introduce me to his family. He says he loves me too much to share me with anyone. Still... he always makes me feel so beautiful.

# THE CURSE OF BEAUTY

Can someone please tell me why it hurts so much to be this beautiful?

All my life, I've been alienated because of how I look. So many guys want to get with me—but they're too intimidated by my beauty.

I try everything to avoid attention. But even on my rough days, they can't take their eyes off me.

Now I understand—beauty can be a curse.

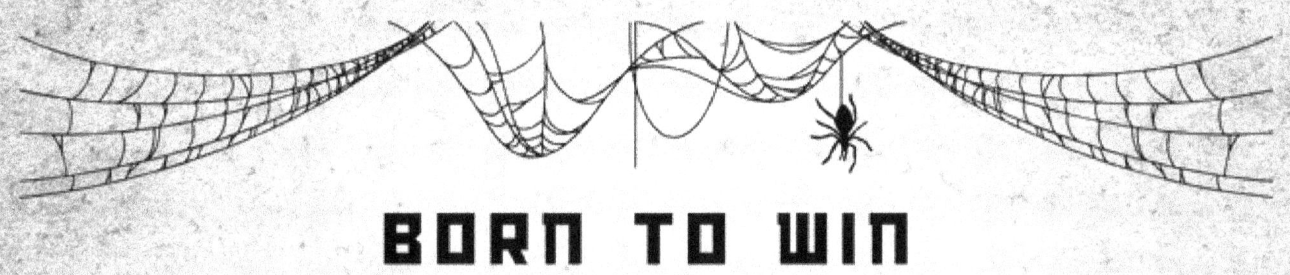

# BORN TO WIN

My sister and I have won so many beauty pageants, it's not even funny. When other girls hear that we're entering, they won't even bother competing. We get it—it's not fair to them. We just embody true beauty.

It's not our fault. We come from good genes.

Sometimes we fight over silly things—like who spends too long in front of the mirror, or who's prettier. Just normal sibling rivalry.

But when we go out, we stick together. We have to. It takes both of us to handle all the haters.

# BEAUTY THROUGH THE HEART

My name is Dieula. I'm twenty-five and teach elementary education. My students all love me, and their parents are very supportive. I don't know why, but starting out was very difficult. As a child, the school recommended that I be homeschooled. I felt isolated learning everything at home, but in time, I got used to it.

As I got older, I pleaded with my parents to enroll me in public school. They kept telling me I was so beautiful that other students would be jealous. I couldn't understand. Yes, I always knew I was beautiful—because I had a beautiful heart. I thought that should be the most important part of a person.

When I would go shopping with my mom, people always stared, as if there was something wrong with me. My mom would just tell me I was special and leave it at that. I spent a lot of time alone, reading romantic novels and looking in the mirror, pretending I was a beautiful princess. I dreamed of meeting my prince someday. Surely, he would come and be my happy ending.

One night, I had a dream. An old, beautiful, wise woman told me, "Dieula, live your life through your heart and always know your true beauty." That dream empowered me to wake up and break through all the obstacles that had held me back. No longer would I live an isolated life.

During high school, I became very popular. I was chosen Prom Queen my senior year. People were attracted to my heart. Attending university opened more doors, and I graduated with high honors. I've been teaching for three years now, and it has been a very pleasurable and rewarding experience.

I've learned that it's better to see beauty with your heart rather than your eyes.

ESTEBAN

# BURIED SOUL

Sometimes we have to look deeper to find the soul of a person who has been buried in darkness, imprisoned in a world so cold. Is there anyone who can see her and realize that her heart beats and longs to be recognized? She yearns to speak—but only growls. Whatever sweetness she once had is now covered in layers of anguish, heartache, and despair.

Will this be her ending—or will the sun shine down on her with the promise of a new day?

# A FLEETING MOMENT

I know you know me. Remember that wonderful night we spent together? You kept telling me how beautiful I was, and how you never wanted the night to end. Oh, what a night—the candlelight, and the aroma that filled the air.

Sadly, nothing lasts forever. The moment I wanted to hold on to was fleeting. I opened my eyes, and you were gone.

ESTEBAN

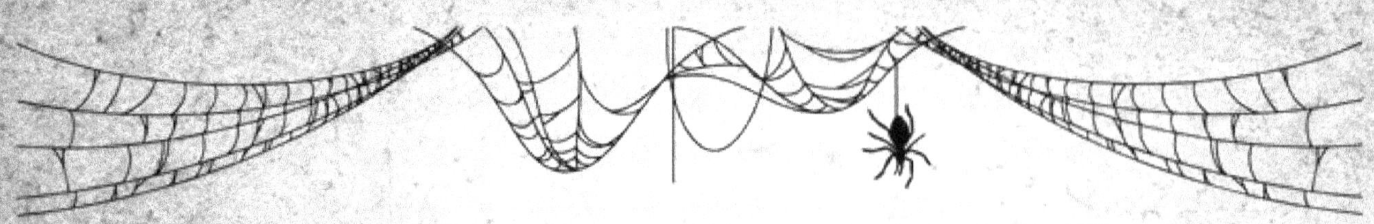

# EYES OF PARADISE

Look into my beautiful eyes and see that you will always belong to me. It took you a long time traveling this world before you came across everything you ever wanted in a woman. I am that woman. I was created just for you.

Everything you've ever desired, you will find in me. You don't have to dream anymore. My unique beauty will bring you satisfaction beyond your wildest fantasies. Each day, you will wake up thanking God for bringing me into your life.

It may sound like I'm bragging or being overconfident—but that is not the case. I know what I know. And if you just take the courage to look into my beautiful green eyes, I will take you to the land of Paradise.

My dear, Heaven is waiting for you.

ESTEBAN

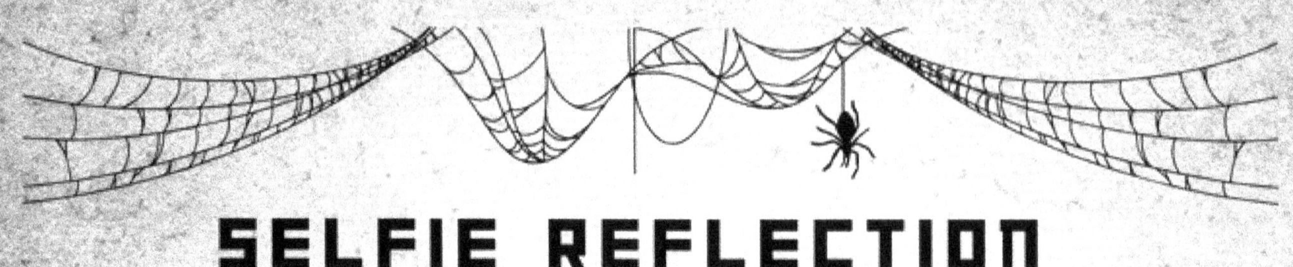

# SELFIE REFLECTION

I really love taking selfies. They always show my best side, and I'm never alone. I think I'm becoming addicted to myself. All I can see—and all I want to see—is me. As long as I'm able to take selfies, I'll never be alone.

ESTEBAN

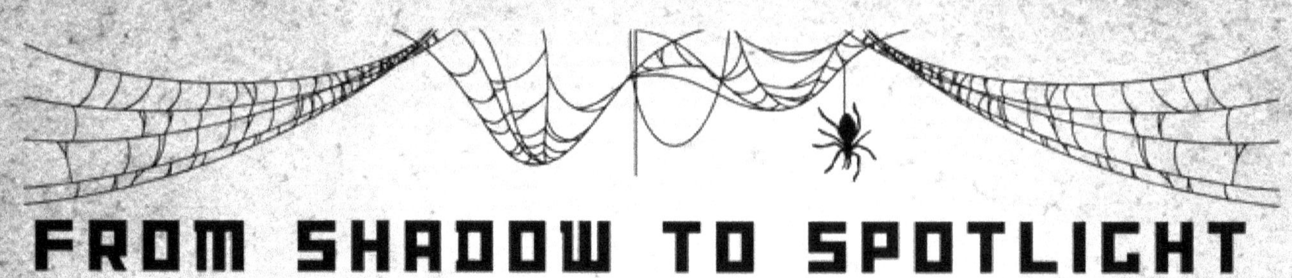

# FROM SHADOW TO SPOTLIGHT

I love my flaming eyes and red hair. I know I can get any man I want. Who could resist a hot babe like me? Don't knock it until you try it—I will truly rock your world.

I was once a shy little girl, afraid of my own shadow. Then a bolt of lightning hit me, and I was never the same. Now, I make use of every moment. No moss will grow under my feet. I dance to the rhythm and get down to the funky beat.

Genesis

# THE REUNION OF QUEENS

We are so happy to be back together again. After graduating from college, we all went our separate ways. We promised that our special bond would not be broken, and we set a date for a five-year reunion.

Well, here we are in Costa Rica, having the time of our lives. Everyone considered us a bourgeois clique on campus and stayed clear of us. It was so bad that when we walked into the cafeteria, library, student union, or any social gathering, everyone would make an exit. Talk about extreme haters.

We didn't mind their leaving; it just meant more food and drink for us. We literally ran the campus. How cool was that? We even had our own sorority, Delta Suka Phi. We had the best party house on campus—especially during Halloween. We always won first prize for originality.

Sisters in this photo are (from left to right): Ana Gomez, Rosalia Trejo, Sallie Mendenez, Nannette Marquez, and Lia Jimenez. We still look good and never have a problem getting attention. Life ain't nothing but a party.

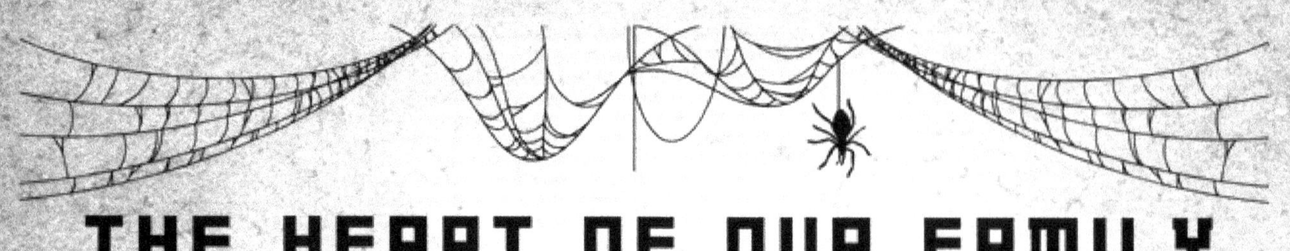

# THE HEART OF OUR FAMILY

Here we all are celebrating Grandma's ninety-eighth birthday. She's still as beautiful as she was seventy years ago. A soul like hers only gets better with time. She has been the rock in our family. Through her wisdom, we have all learned what really matters in life.

She taught us how to hold our heads up during difficult times, not to let mistreatment affect our spirit, and to always turn the other cheek. Although we didn't understand some of the things she said, we obeyed her words—resulting in us being blessed.

Everyone should have a grandmother like Grandma Maebelle. She made the world a better place.

ESTEBAN

# ANCIENT EYES, ETERNAL WISDOM

I am the King of the World. That's how I see myself. I have been on this earth since the beginning of time. Through evolution, I have seen dinosaurs become extinct while crocodiles continue to thrive. I have seen volcanoes erupt and form new mountains and islands. I have seen great floods create new continents. Yes, I have also witnessed the evolution of humanity.

Through all that I have seen, I realize that our survival is not based on strength or intelligence but on one's ability to adapt.

ESTEBAN

# VOICES FROM INFINITY

We are members of infinity. We outnumber you, and our population keeps growing minute by minute. Even as we write this, many are joining us. It is unfortunate how fear becomes part of the inevitable journey into the unknown.

When we left, all the things that chained us down to the daily rigors of life no longer mattered. Driving two hours to get to work and two hours back home. Worrying if you'll have enough to pay the mortgage and buy groceries. Arguing about the separation between church and state. Watching the rich get richer. Wondering if a president should uphold the Constitution. Asking when World War Three will begin.

The myriad issues confronting our lives today will continue tomorrow—with or without you. Most likely, they will evolve and become more complex. That's for another generation to worry about.

Freedom's just another word for nothing left to lose.

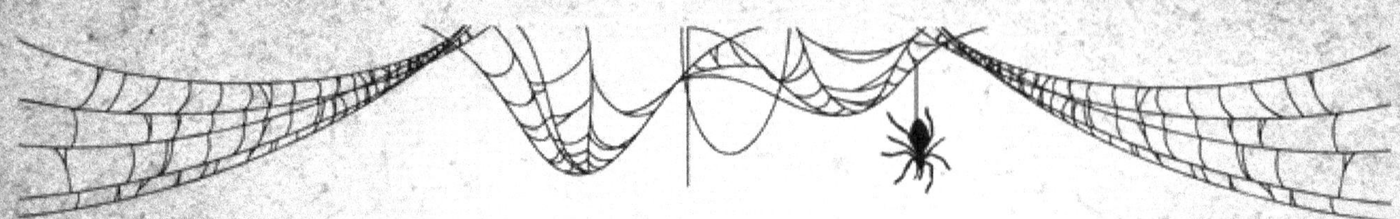

# BORN OF STORMS, GUIDED BY STORIES

I was born under a beautiful dark sky with lightning bolts celebrating my birth. As the winds howled out my name, I could hear the echoes of those who had come before me.

What would be my fate? Was I destined to become a legend? Did I have a purpose in this life? As I started my journey, there were so many unknowns. As I traveled this world, I met numerous beautiful people. They were not movie stars, professional athletes, models, or politicians. They were just regular people trying to make the best of their lives.

Some had reached the dream of owning a home, while others found a home under the bridge. Each had a story to tell—of victories and failures. As I listened to their stories, it became clear to me that our true profession should be finding our way to ourselves.

ESTEBAN

# THE BEAUTY WITHIN ME

My name is Fatima. Believe it or not, I am only twenty years of age. To look at me, I'm sure you wonder how I stay so beautiful. Despite the hardships of my life, I keep a song in my heart, and I love spreading joy wherever I go.

It saddens me when people reject joy and replace it with fear. What could they possibly see in me that would result in fear? They don't understand that I am all about peace, love, and harmony.

I pray that someday people will stop judging by the look of the cover and take a deeper look into one's soul.

STEBAN

# A MOTHER'S PRAYER

Dear Lord, please watch over my beautiful child and protect him from the cruelty of the world. Dress him in armor so that no evil can penetrate his soul. Let him know how beautiful he is and that you created him to do great things.

When I leave this earth, I want him to carry on and do good works in your name. Give him wisdom, for in wisdom there is true beauty and love. Shield him from darkness, which destroys the spirit. Lift him up, Lord, and let him know that he is part of your kingdom.

ESTEBAN

# SURVIVORS OF THE TRADE

We are ancestors of the Global Trade. Our beauty lies in the fact that we have survived man's inhumanity to man, yet our spirit has remained strong. Stripped from our native land, families separated and shipped all over the globe, stacked on ships like animals, many dying and thrown overboard, and considered only to be three-fifths human—these are just a few of the hardships of Global Trade.

Through all the unimaginable abuse, our spirit was empowered through songs from the heart. We definitely understand why the caged bird sings.

ESTEBAN